GRAMMY & SAMMY

GRAMMY & SAMMY

written & illustrated by
LISA PASSEN

HENRY HOLT AND COMPANY
New York

Published by Henry Holt and Company, Inc.,
115 West 18th Street, New York, New York 10011.
Published in Canada by Fitzhenry & Whiteside Limited,
195 Allstate Parkway, Markham, Ontario L3R 4T8.

Library of Congress Cataloging-in-Publication Data
Passen, Lisa.
Grammy & Sammy / written and illustrated by Lisa Passen.
Summary: Grammy comes to live with a girl and her parents but does
not get along with Sammy the cat.
ISBN 0-8050-1415-2
[1. Grandmothers—Fiction.   2. Cats—Fiction.]   I. Title.
II. Title: Grammy and Sammy.
PZ7.P26937Gr   1990
[E]—dc20   90-32068

Printed in the United States of America
on acid-free paper.

First Edition

1   3   5   7   9   10   8   6   4   2

Dedicated to
my husband Bruce

Things were real
nice at our house.

Until my grandmother came.
Not to visit.
To live.
FOREVER.

Mom said that Grammy had been alone
way too long, ever since her poodle Fifi
and Grandpa were gone.

I thought it would be fun
having Grammy live with us.
I love her a lot.

But Sammy thought different.
Sammy is my cat.

Grammy sat down on
Sammy's favorite chair.
Sammy arched his back
and hissed at Grammy.
"Filthy beast!"
Grammy shouted.
"My Fifi was never
so disrespectful!"

I knew we were
in for trouble.

Sammy shared my bedroom.
Now Grammy would be sharing it too.

Grammy said her Fifi NEVER
set foot in a bedroom. She
said it was unhealthy to have
a filthy animal sleeping in
the same room as you.

Why did she keep calling
Sammy filthy? He was
ALWAYS cleaning himself.

But Sammy couldn't
sleep with me anymore.

The next day Grammy
and I went into town.

We mailed some letters.

We shared a deluxe
peanut-butter fudge
ice-cream soda.

And we
looked
at the
stores.

While we were waiting for the bus home, we stopped in front of a really, really wonderful store.

In one week it would be my birthday. I looked in the store window. Then I looked at Grammy. I didn't think she noticed.

As soon as we walked in the door at
home, Sammy ran away. Oh, why can't
Grammy and Sammy be friends?

At dinner that night Sammy wouldn't even come in the kitchen until Grammy left the table.

And again he didn't sleep in our bedroom.

Before I left for school the next day,
I whispered to Sammy, "Be a good cat
and make friends with Grammy."

But when I came
home later, Mom
told me to be
very quiet.
"Grammy has
had a hard day.

"Sammy got into Grammy's things.
He played with her clothes.
He tore up some photographs. . . .
And worst of all, he
opened her purse and
made a mess!

"When she saw
what he had done,
Grammy chased
after him.

"Sammy jumped up on a bookcase, knocked it over,
landed on Grammy's head, and pulled her wig off."

"Grammy wears a WIG?"
I screamed.
"Forget about Grammy's wig,"
Mom said. "Just behave in
front of her. And . . .
Sammy must stay
outside from now on."

I didn't think that was very fair. Grammy didn't understand that Sammy just wanted to play with her. Cats are like that.

So Sammy had to stay outside.

The night before my birthday, it started to rain. Sammy was outside.

Then it started to rain hard. And then it really poured!
There was lightning and thunder. The windows rattled.

Poor Sammy. I bet Grammy was happy.

But she wasn't.
She looked kind of funny.
She walked back and forth.
She went from window to window.
She went to the front door.
She went to the side door.
She went to the back door.
And then I heard her.

She was calling. "Sammy! Sammy! Where are you, Sammy?"

I heard a little cry, and then Sammy came running in the door, soaking wet. He shook and shook. "Stupid cat!" said Grammy. "Don't you know enough to come in out of the rain?"

Sammy purred, and rubbed against Grammy's leg.
Mom and Dad looked surprised.

We celebrated my birthday with
a big purple-and-pink cake.
Mom and Dad gave me a very nice
blue sweater and a doll with
long red hair.

. . . And Grammy gave me and Sammy
a stuffed toy mouse!

Grammy said, "I would have gotten
you something bigger, but I lost
my pension check."

I knew what really happened to
Grammy's pension check, but I
didn't say anything . . .

and neither did Grammy!